Aladdin Books
Macmillan Publishing Company
866 Third Avenue, New York, NY 10022

First Aladdin Books Edition 1988

Printed in Singapore

ISBN 0-689-71230-8

Dear Zoo

Rod Campbell

ALADDIN BOOKS
MACMILLAN PUBLISHING COMPANY
NEW YORK

I wrote to the zoo
to send me a pet.
They sent me an ...

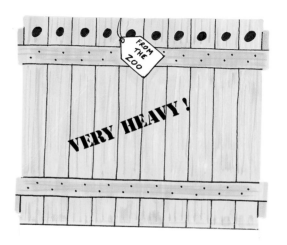

He was too big!
I sent him back.

So they sent me a . . .

He was too tall!
I sent him back.

So they sent me a . . .

He was too fierce!
I sent him back.

So they sent me a . . .

He was too grumpy!
I sent him back.

So they sent me a . . .

He was too scary!
I sent him back.

So they sent me a . . .

He was too naughty!
I sent him back.

So they thought
very hard, and
sent me a . . .

He was perfect!
I kept him.